THE RIDDLE GIRL

An Anglo-Saxon Story

By *Sheila Lane*

Illustrated by Gillian Marklew

GW00385237

ANGLIA *young* BOOKS

First published in 1996
by Anglia Young Books
Durhams Farmhouse
Ickleton
Saffron Walden, Essex CB10 1SR

Illustrations by Gillian Marklew

British Library Cataloguing-in-Publication Data

A catalogue record for this book is available from the
British Library

ISBN 1 871173 55 8

Typeset in Palatino by Goodfellow & Egan, Cambridge
and printed in Great Britain by
Ashford Colour Press, Gosport, Hampshire

CHAPTER ONE

Alda was tired of looking after the pigs. It was Springtime and she wanted to hunt for birds' nests.

She and her father drove their pigs down to the marsh every day. There the little herd could burrow in the soft earth for roots and acorns. If she let them wander into the water, her father would beat her. He'd done it often enough.

She gave a quick glance over her shoulder to where he was collecting wood on the edge of the forest. Very softly she began creeping through the reeds to where a bird was flying in and out under the leaves of a willow tree. There might be a nest – and young ones.

'You idle brat! Where are you?'

Picking up a stick, Alda ran out from the reeds.

'I'm here, father! I went to get a stick.'

Two of the pigs had strayed down to the water. Alda threw a handful of pebbles into the stream. Startled by the sound of the stones hitting the water, the pigs scuttled back to the herd.

As her father walked towards her, Alda rubbed her shoulders. They were still sore from yesterday's blows. She began to tremble. Would she escape punishment this time? The pigs hadn't gone right into the water and her father couldn't have seen her by the willow tree.

Looking up at the sky he said, 'I'm taking this wood back to the hut. Bring the pigs home when the sun is over the willow tree, girl. Don't take your eyes off them for one moment – do you hear?'

He was going! Alda felt a huge surge of relief. Ever since her brother, Alfric, had been sold to the thane chief last winter, her father's temper had grown harsher. Every time he looked at her, Alda knew that he was comparing her with Alfric. Forty shillings the thanes had paid for her brother and with the money her father had bought some flour, a goat and this little herd of pigs. That was how they'd survived the bitter winter.

It was boring watching pigs, but she had the birds flying over the marsh for company. Alda loved birds. Another warbler flew in under the hanging branches of the willow tree. This one had a worm in its beak. So there must be a nest.

Forgetting the pigs, Alda tiptoed towards the tree and quietly pulled the branches apart. There, nuzzling close to each other, in a nest of twigs and moss, were five little fledglings, all brown and soft and warm. She smiled as the mother bird shared a fat worm between her young ones.

'Arrh! Yarra!'

Along the path by the stream a gang of young boys ran towards the pigs. But Alda didn't hear them. She was gazing at the little birds as the mother flew out from under the leaves on another hunt for food. She sighed. How hard that mother had to work to keep her children fed.

Suddenly, she heard a pig squeal. She spun

round and saw the boys. They had circled the marsh and were driving the pigs towards the stream.

Alda stumbled towards them crying, 'Stop! Stop! They're my pigs! *Stop!*'

The leader of the young thieves turned round, tossing his long, red hair back over his shoulders. 'Come and get them, *pig-girl*,' he jeered.

It was Wulfwin, the thane chief's son. Alda had seen him once before. It was when the family had gone to the thanes' village last winter to sell her brother. The boy with long, red hair had laughed at her mother's tears when Alfric was led away and now he was laughing again. He called out to his gang, 'Yarra! Yarra! Get the pigs away!' And the boys, firing pointed sticks from their rough bows, drove the little herd back towards the thanes' village.

Alda began to run after them. 'Stop! Stop!' she cried and then stood still. It was useless. The family's precious pigs had been stolen. Her mouth went dry. Hadn't her brother been sold for those pigs? Hadn't her mother wept and said that it was blood money, just forty shillings for a son? And now there was no Alfric and no pigs.

She climbed onto a boulder and gazed after the thieves. She could do nothing on her own. Tears trickled down her pale cheeks.

Then she saw that one of the boys was walking a distance behind the others, carrying what looked like some of the thanes' bows. As this boy walked, his head rocked from side to side. That was how Alfric used to walk – slowly, with his head rocking. Could the boy be Alfric? Could it be that Alfric was now Wulfwin's slave and had to follow him everywhere?

Alda stared at the rocking head. It had a shock of dark hair, like her mother's. Curling her hand round her mouth she called his name: 'Alfric! Alfric!'

For a moment the boy stopped. Then, shifting the bundle of bows onto his other shoulder, he walked on towards the village.

Alda shivered. Now she would have to go back home and tell her father what had happened. She turned away from the marsh and ran along the rough track that led to the family hut.

Scratched and breathless, she reached the clearing and saw her father stacking wood outside their hut door. For a moment she stood still and stared at her father's bent back. Even when he stood up he was still bent over from the long hours he'd spent working in the cold, wet forest. With shaking hands she pushed the long strands of damp hair from her face and called out, 'Father! Father!'

He looked up. 'What are you doing back here? The pigs! Where are they?'

Alda stumbled forward. 'Father! Believe me! It was not my fault.'

Arm raised, her father strode towards her. 'Where are the pigs?'

'Gone!' It was only a whisper.

'You useless creature! What have you done?'

Alda put up her arms, trying to protect her head from the blows that rained down across her shoulders. 'No! No! No!'

Her father's fist struck the back of her head and she fell forwards onto the ground. Looking up she cried: 'I … I … was watching them … I swear I was. Like arrows from a bow they came.'

'Arrows! What arrows?' The man stared down at his daughter. '*What arrows*? You talk in riddles, girl.'

'It was Wulfwin and a gang of young thanes from the village. They drove our pigs away with stones and pointed sticks.' She staggered to her feet. 'Mother!' she cried. 'Mother!'

A woman, holding a wooden bowl, came to the door of the hut. 'What have you done child?'

'It's the pigs, mother.' Alda held up her tear-stained face. 'They've been stolen.'

'Our pigs – *stolen*! Who took them?

'Some young thanes. I was watching over the pigs, down where the warblers make their nests in Spring'

'Birds! Birds!' Alda's father sat down heavily on a pile of fire-wood and put his head in his hands. 'It's always birds with her. She says the pigs were driven away by Wulfwin and his gang from the village.' He looked up hopelessly. 'What can we do against our lords?'

The woman wiped her face on her sleeve and leaned wearily against the wooden planks of the hut door. 'We can do nothing,' she said. 'We poor churls can do nothing against the thanes.'

Alda stretched out her hands. 'Father! Hear me!'

'Shut your mouth, girl! There's nothing we can do.'

'There is! There is!' Alda spoke urgently. 'I can

go to the Chief and tell him what Wulfwin did.'

Her mother's mouth dropped open. 'Go to lord Godric, child! You can't do that.'

'I can! I can!'

'You! Go to lord Godric!' Her father looked at Alda scornfully. 'Who would believe *you*?'

'But father! They say that lord Godric is a fair man. They call him Godric the Good. Last winter, when we took Alfric to the thanes' village ...'

At Alfric's name anger flashed across her father's face. 'Don't talk of Alfric, girl. He was slow, but ...' For a moment the churl's mouth trembled as he remembered that dreadful day when he had sold his son. Then he went on, 'I had to do it. We were starving. Besides, he is well placed and eats meat every day.' He gazed bitterly at his wife and daughter. 'When did I last have meat in my belly? Even the thanes' dogs eat better than we poor churls.'

Alda pulled at her mother's arm and spoke in a whisper. 'Mother! When I was down at the marsh I saw a boy like Alfric. I think it was him.'

Her mother stared at her.

'*Think*, you say! You must *know* your own brother, child. *Was* it Alfric?'

Alda shook her head.

'I can't be sure. This boy was walking behind Wulfwin and his gang. He walked slowly, with his head rocking, just like Alfric.'

Her father looked up.

'You could have called to him.'

'I did Father. But he didn't answer. He was too far away.'

Her father sighed. 'You're useless!'

'I'm not! I'm not! And I can do something. I can go to lord Godric.'

Her mother nodded. 'What do you say, husband?'

He shrugged. 'Who would believe her?'

Alda said, 'Perhaps Wulfwin and his gang grew tired of their sport. Perhaps they went back to their village and left the pigs to wander in the forest.'

Her father got to his feet.

'Well, I suppose there's a chance. Tether the goat inside the hut, wife. You, girl! Help me to roll the keeper stone against the door.'

That done, they set off along the track that led down to the marsh.

CHAPTER TWO

It was still light when they reached the marsh. Alda waded into the little stream and bathed her scratched legs.

Suddenly she gave a cry: 'Father! Over here! Look!'

Her father came and squatted beside her on the muddy bank. 'Footprints,' he said. 'So the young thanes *were* here.'

Alda looked up at him. 'You see!' she said. 'There were so many of them.'

'Aye, girl,' said her father. 'It was not all your fault.'

She ran along the path. 'There are more here.' Then she stood still and gazed towards the thanes' settlement. 'They've taken our pigs into the village. I'm sure of it.'

'You may be right, girl,' said her father, 'but those brats will have them in their own swine pens by now.'

Alda's mother shook her clenched fist. 'Husband!' Without our pigs we shall starve. We must go to Godric. It's our right to be heard.'

'True! It's our right, but would we be believed?' Unsure, Alda's mother and father stood together by the stream.

But Alda was already walking steadily along the path towards the thanes' village.

Alda's mother clasped her husband's arm. 'She can't go to that place alone. She's only a child. Stop her!'

They ran and caught up with Alda as she reached the ditch that surrounded the stockade – the wooden fence protecting the settlement.

'Wait, girl!' Her father pulled her behind a clump of osier saplings. 'Lord Godric will be in his Meeting House after nightfall. That will be the time to try and tell him.'

But Alda was impatient. 'Can't we go now?' she asked.

'No!' Her father pointed to the other side of the ditch. 'We must get over to the bank and stay under the shadow of the fence until it's dark. We can't go over the bridge or someone will see us and send us away.'

They waded into the water and tried to climb up the steep side of the bank. But it was slippery. With every step they slithered back, down into the stagnant water, splattering their legs with green slime.

Alda looked along to where a rough bridge led to a gap in the stockade. Somehow they would have to get through that gap. But first they must cross the ditch. Seeing an elder branch hanging over the ditch she struggled towards it, but it was just out of reach. She crouched under the bough, jumped up, grasped it with both hands and heaved herself up onto the top of the bank. Her father followed and then her mother. Breathless, covered with slime and dung from the water, they leant back against the stockade.

Footsteps!

Through the gathering darkness, they saw the figure of a boy, bent double under a load of fire-wood, trudging slowly over the bridge.

Alda clutched her mother's arm. 'It's Alfric,' she breathed.

Putting her hands to her head, her mother let out a cry:'*Alfric*!'

Alda turned to her father. 'You see! It *was* Alfric down by the marsh. I'm sure of it now. He'll tell us where they took the pigs.'

She called out: 'Alfric! Along here! On the bank.'

The boy, startled, dropped his load and looked round. When he saw his family huddled under the elder tree, he looked terrified. 'What are you doing here?' he whispered.

His father spoke quietly. 'It's the pigs! They've been stolen.'

Alda interrupted: 'It was Wulfwin.'

'*Wulfwin*!' At the sound of Wulfwin's name Alfric looked even more frightened.

'Yes! Wulfwin! I saw him.'

Alfric shrugged and shook his head, but Alda persisted. 'Alfric! You were nearby. You must have seen what happened.'

'No!'

'You did! You did! Wulfwin and his gang drove them away just ahead of you.'

'Alfric!' It was his father who was speaking now. 'We're going to see lord Godric.'

'*No!*' said Alfric urgently. 'You can't do that. No churl can come into the village after night-fall. It's the law.'

'Alfric,' his mother pleaded. 'Help us, my son. You are our blood. Our pigs have been taken!'

'I can't!' Alfric spoke roughly. 'Besides, I'm late already.'

Sensing that he was about to go, Alda caught hold of an elder bough and swung herself side-ways over the ditch. She landed on the bridge and stood in front of Alfric, her arms out-stretched.

'Listen, brother! Wulfwin and his gang stole our pigs. They're in the village. She clutched his shoulders. 'Where are they?'

'I don't know. Go away. Someone will see you!'

'You do know!' persisted Alda. 'You must do. Tell me where they'll be.'

Alfric pulled away from her and pointed towards some huts apart from the others, just visible in the fading light. 'Somewhere that way. I don't know. Most likely they've been penned in the hollow huts that lie behind the weaving sheds.'

With that Alfric picked up his load. 'I must go,' he muttered. 'I'm late already. There'll be trouble.'

'*Alfric!*' his mother gave one last despairing wail.

'Leave him, woman,' insisted his father. 'We must go to lord Godric. It's the only way.' He turned to Alda. 'Listen, girl. We must wait outside until lord Godric's at his Ale Board. Then we must to to the door of the Meeting House and tell him our grievance.'

'No, father! I'm going to search those hollow huts before it's too dark.'

'I tell you, *no*! That could make trouble for us all.'

But Alda was on the bridge and out of her father's reach.

'I'm going to find our pigs,' she called and disappeared inside the thanes' village.

CHAPTER THREE

The thanes' weaving huts, open at one side, lay at the far side of the settlement. In the half-light Alda could just see the outline of the women's looms. Alfric had said that the pigs were likely to be in the hollow huts. What had he meant? All huts would be empty in the middle. Then she noticed a cluster of low shacks made of rough sticks, half open at the top.

She ran lightly over the grass, hardly daring to hope that the precious pigs were so near. She reached the first hut, wrenched two of the sticks apart and peered inside. Whimpering sounds! 'Goats,' she muttered in disappointment. 'Just goats!' But she'd disturbed them and they began to bleat more loudly.

A voice called, 'Who's there?'

The goats' cries had alerted someone. The huts were low, no higher than Alda herself, so there was nowhere to hide. She ran to the next one, crouched down behind it and then stretched herself flat out on the ground.

Her heart thumped wildly. 'Don't find me,' she whispered to herself. 'Please don't find me.'

As she lay there, scarcely daring to breathe, she heard the two sticks being hammered back into the ground. Then all was quiet again.

Very slowly Alda raised her head and pushed herself up on her hands. She peered through the darkness. There was no-one there. Then she heard faint snuffling sounds. They were coming from the next hut. She crawled towards it on her hands and knees, pushed her hands between some rotting sticks at the bottom and peered inside.

'*Pigs*! Our pigs,' she said in triumph, 'sleeping.'

She looked back over her shoulder. It was quiet everywhere, but she'd have to be quick. At first the sticks refused to give way. Then, with her foot, she managed to ease one out of

the ground and lift it upwards. She pushed against the side of the hut and, without warning, other sticks gave way and she fell inside.

The startled pigs, wakened from their sleep, squealed in alarm and huddled together at the back of the hut. Alda picked up a broken stick and began to drive them onto the grass outside.

'Sh-roo!' she hissed at them. 'Sh-roo!'

The dazed pigs looked round, not knowing where to go.

'*Sh-roo*!' Alda's voice grew louder as she urged them round to the back of the weaving sheds with her stick.

'Arrh! Yarra!' … Who was that?

She knew that voice. She'd heard it that morning down at the marsh. It was Wulfwin, the chief's son. Terrified, she held her breath and flattened herself against the wall of one of the weaving sheds.

'Don't let him find me,' she whispered.

'Arrh! Yarra!' Someone's there,' shouted the voice.

More figures came looming out of the darkness. 'Arrh! Yarra!' they roared.

In the uproar, the pigs scattered, some running round and round the weaving sheds in panic, others trotting back to the safety of the hollow hut.

Alda dropped her stick and darted round to the open front of the shed. From one of the looms hung a length of half woven cloth. A hiding place! She could hear the boys running after the pigs and trying to round them up in the darkness. Perhaps they would herd them up and drive them back to the hut. Then she'd be able to get back to the bridge.

Then she saw him!

A pale shaft of moonlight suddenly illuminated the tall figure, with shoulder length red hair, standing and staring at the loom where she was hiding. It was Wulfwin.

He strode towards the loom.

'It's the pig-girl!' he shouted. 'She's in here.'

He grasped Alda's long hair and pulled her, screaming, out onto the grass.

'Got you, pig-girl!' He laughed as he grabbed her hands and pinned them behind her back.

'Let me go!' But it was a forlorn cry. She knew that there was no hope of escape now.

'Over here, boys! I've got the churl.'

Moments later she was surrounded by young thanes. 'Dirty churl! Dirty churl!' they jeered.

'*Leave her*!'

Alda's father and mother had come running into the village when they'd heard their daughter's cries.

'The girl's done no harm. Leave her alone.'

Wulfwin let go of Alda's arms, lurched forwards and struck Alda's father to the ground.

'Who are you to tell me what to do?' he roared.

'The girl's my daughter.'

Wulfwin laughed. 'Who are you to tell me what to do, pig-girl's father?'

Alda's mother ran forward and clutched Wulfwin's arm. 'Our pigs were taken.'

Wulfwin shook her off angrily. 'Don't touch me, you dirty churl.' He spat in her face. 'Pigs! All of you.'

Alda's father stumbled to his feet. He was shaking, partly in anger and partly in fear. 'We've come to speak to lord Godric.'

'My father!' For a moment Wulfwin sounded alarmed. 'You've no business with my father. And you've no business in the village after night-fall. Don't you churls know anything of the law?'

'We have our rights. Lord Godric is a fair man. He'll hear us.'

Wulfwin's face darkened. 'You've no business with my father. So, get out, all of you.'

Alda clenched her fists. 'And you've no business to take our pigs. I'm going to tell lord Godric what happened.'

'Tell him, will you, pig-girl?' Wulfwin's face was ugly. He turned to his companions. 'Tie them up, boys. We'll take them to the Great Oak Tree. Then we'll see what they still want to tell the Chief.'

And the three were dragged away to the Great Oak which stood outside the Meeting House.

CHAPTER FOUR

It was hot in the Meeting House. There was a strong smell of roasting meat, ale and unwashed bodies. Smoke from the clay hearth in the middle of the hall wafted over the wooden benches up to the hole in the thatched roof.

Lord Godric sat at the Ale Board with his thanes. The men ate greedily, throwing bones to the hungry hunting dogs lying at their feet and gulping strong ale from their drinking horns.

The thane chief was a giant of a man with thick, red hair and a heavy, curling beard. His woollen cloak was flung back from his broad shoulders and pinned on one side with a round, jewelled brooch. His wife, Hilde, her blonde hair neatly braided beneath a linen cowl, refilled her husband's drinking horn with mead. From her waist dangled a set of bronze girdle-hangers. They were a sign of Hilde's position and showed that she was in charge of stores.

Serving women, dressed in ankle length gowns of roughly woven cloth, carried pitchers of ale and brought fresh bread and meat to the Board.

Lord Godric, his hunger satisfied, banged on the Ale Board with his great fist. 'Where's my Riddler?' he called.

An old man, with straggly white hair framing his lined face and dressed in a long, blue tunic looked up. Gildas had been in the service of the last chief and had known Godric since he was a boy.

Slinging his six-stringed harp across his shoulders, he hobbled forward. 'What will you hear from my word-hoard tonight, master?' he said.

Godric smiled kindly at his old friend. 'Put us to the test, Gildas. Give us a new riddle.'

The Riddler settled himself back on his stool and began:

'Open your ears
and tell me,
if you can,
what it is …'

He was interrupted by a commotion at the door of the Meeting House. There were cries of, 'Out, boy! *Get out!*' as Alfric, the young slave, tried to push his way forward to the Ale Board.

'My lord Godric!' he cried, flinging himself onto the clay floor. 'My lord … out there … at the Great Oak … there's … there's … trouble.'

Godric beckoned the boy forward. 'Come here. What have you seen?'

Alfric got to his feet. 'Out there, at the Great Oak.' He paused and looked around at the thanes' faces.'There's a poor family from the forest. They've been tied up … and …' Alfric bowed his head and brushed a hand across his eyes.

'Go on, boy,' said Godric.

Alfric began to sob. 'They're being tormented.'

The Chief's wife asked: 'What can churls from the forest be doing in the village at this time of night?'

Godric nodded. 'They know that it's against our law.'

His wife shrugged. 'They must have done some wrong.'

Godric turned to a thane messenger. 'Go and see what's happening,' he ordered.

As the messenger hurried out, Wulfwin edged his way into the Meeting House and stood beside his mother. She smiled on her favourite.

'You're late, my son,' she said. 'Where have you been all day?'

Wulfwin scowled. 'About my business, mother.'

Godric looked across at this son. 'And what business brought you late and red-faced to our gathering, Wulfwin?'

Wulfwin tossed his head. 'Just some young men's games, father,' he said defiantly.

Alfric, standing beside the Riddler murmured, 'Games! Games, he calls it.'

Wulfwin's mother looked anxiously at the chief. 'Young men must have their sport, husband,' she said.

Lord Godric stroked his beard. He looked long and hard at Wulfwin. 'What have you been doing?' he asked.

Wulfwin shifted his feet uneasily. 'We were at spear play, father.'

'Ah!' Lord Godric looked pleased. 'One day my own sword will be handed down to you, my son. You must be ready.'

The messenger returned. 'My lord Godric! A family of forest churls are tied up to the Great Oak out there. It seems they were tormented by some of our young thanes who ran away when I began to question them.' He nodded towards Alfric, who was cowering behind the Riddler. 'The boy was right to bring you word.'

'Young thanes, you say.' Lord Godric sighed. 'Bring the churls in.'

All eyes turned towards the door as Alda, her father and her mother, were dragged into the hall. Alda's face was white and streaked with mud and tears and her poor, rough gown was covered with animal dung. Her mother, shaking with fear, her head bowed, stumbled and fell onto the clay floor.

Godric looked closely at the man who stood

before him, covered in filth, but head held high. 'Aren't you the father of the boy I bought last winter?' He pointed at Alfric, hiding behind the Riddler.

'I am, my lord, but I've not come here to speak to you about Alfric.'

'Then what brought you into the village after night-fall?' went on Godric. 'You know the law.'

Alda leaned forward and put her hands on the edge of the Ale Board. 'Please my lord,' she said. 'We've come for our pigs.'

Her mother tugged at Alda's skirt. 'Hush, girl! Let your father speak.'

'No, mother,' she said. 'I must tell lord Godric what happened at the marsh today.'

Godric nodded. 'Go on, girl.'

'Our pigs were stolen by your young thanes, my lord.'

Her father hissed: 'Hush, girl'

'No, father!' She turned and pointed to Wulfwin. '*He* saw … *he* was there.'

Wulfwin lunged towards Alda. Prodding her with his finger, he said, 'Lies, churl, lies! Don't

you know that Thor strikes dumb anyone whose tongue speaks lies?'

Alda gripped the table with both hands. 'My lord Godric,' she cried. 'We came here to get our pigs back and tonight your young thanes treated *us* like pigs. We want our rights.'

'What does a girl churl know of rights?' began Wulfwin.

But Alda would not be silenced. 'We were tied up and stoned … and … *look*!' She pointed to her poor clothes, stained with mud and blood. 'Look at me!'

'Enough!' Godric turned to his wife. 'Take them away and let the girl clean herself.'

As the churls were led away, Godric looked hard at Wulfwin. 'Whoever tormented the girl, did wrong,' he said. 'I shall hear more of your part in this, my son.'

CHAPTER FIVE

When Alda was brought back to the Ale Board, lord Godric beckoned her forward.

'Now girl,' he said. 'Tell your story.'

When Alda had told her tale, the chief stroked his beard. 'Don't you know that by coming into the village after night-fall, you and your family have done wrong?'

'But the pigs are our whole living. My brother was *sold* for them. Now, without them, we shall starve.'

Lord Godric leant back, folding his arms. 'You've broken our Saxon law.'

Alda took a deep breath. 'My lord! What is the law for loss of pigs?'

Lord Godric raised his great eyebrows. 'What do you know of Saxon law, girl?'

Alda looked along the Ale Board at the hard faces of the thanes and hung her head.

Wulfwin seized his chance. 'I know our Saxon law, father.' He stepped forward and stood beside Alda. 'Listen, girl:

If a man kills another man, he pays 100 shillings

If a man cuts off another man's nose he pays 60 shillings

If a man cuts off a big toe, he pays 20 shillings

If a man cuts off a little toe …'

Alda could bear it no longer. She raised her pale face and cried, 'What about pigs? Is there no law for pigs?'

Wulfwin laughed. 'No! Nothing for pigs!'

Alda turned to lord Godric. 'My lord! You can have one of my toes for a pig.'

Laughter rang round the Meeting House and Godric banged on the Ale Board.

'I like the girl's spirit,' he said.

Wulfwin scowled. 'The girl's clever. She knows you won't do it.'

The old Riddler, who had been sitting on his stool, walked slowly forward and put a hand under Alda's chin. He gazed at her intently for a few seconds and then looked up at Godric. 'Let's test the girl's cleverness with a riddle, master.'

Godric shook his head. 'She's only a forest girl, Gildas.' He paused. 'But you can try her.'

Alda looked up at the Riddler's kind face and her eyes filled with tears. 'How will he test me?' she thought. 'What will he do?'

Gildas smiled down gently at the frightened girl. 'Do you know riddles, child?'

Alda frowned. 'Are they some kind of trick?'

The Riddler nodded. 'Yes! riddles are tricks. They're tricks with words.'

Lord Godric leant forward over the Ale Board. 'Listen to the Riddler's words, girl. If you can guess the answer to his riddle, you can have a pig.'

'A pig!' Alda's face lit up. 'Then I'll do it, if I can.'

The thanes gathered round and Gildas began:

'Open your ears
and tell me,
if you can,
what it is
that I am:

One snuffling, snorting snout,
one great gobbler,
two listeners,
two lookers,
one great belly
and a curly-whirl.'

Alda clapped her hands. 'I know it! It's a pig.'

'A child's riddle,' Wulfwin spoke angrily.
'That's no test.'

Gildas smiled. 'That's so, Wulfwin. I'll try
another.'

'For another pig?' Alda spoke eagerly.

Lord Godric laughed. 'Yes! For another pig,
but make this one harder, Gildas.'

Gildas began as before:

'Open your ears
and tell me,
if you can,
what it is
that I am:

In my white dress
I float,
like an enchanted boat
on stream and river.

I skim over the water
with neck outstretched, arms thrashing
and then ascend
into the air.

Dare to come near my children
in their home amongst the reeds
and you will hear
my angry hiss.'

Alda shook her head. 'This one is full of tricks,' she said. 'A girl wears a white dress, but it's not a girl.'

'Riddles are *word* tricks,' Gildas said. 'The thing to be guessed is often spoken of as if it is something else. Listen for the clues.' And he recited the riddle again.

Alda counted on her fingers. 'It floats on the water, it flies in the air. Could it be a *bird*?'

Gildas nodded his white head. 'Go on, child.'

Alda looked thoughtful. 'A home in the reeds, so it is a water bird?'

'Yes! Yes!' cried Gildas.

'A bird from the water in a white dress. A white water bird. I know it! A *swan*!'

Old Gildas clapped his hands and the thanes cheered.

Lord Godric banged on the Ale Board. 'Take your two pigs and go, girl.'

Alda's face dropped. '*Two* pigs! But twenty were taken, my lord.'

Wulfwin, unable to keep silent any longer, called out, 'Those pigs weren't marked.'

All eyes turned to Wulfwin.

Lord Godric gazed at his son. 'How do you know that, Wulfwin?'

Wulfwin bit his lip and shifted uneasily beside his mother.

The chief leant forward. 'What do you know about these pigs?'

'Nothing, father!'

'Come and stand beside me!' Godric's voice was angry. 'I think you do, and you'll tell me!'

Hilde, always ready to protect her son, put a

hand on the chief's shoulder. 'He was at sport with his friends, husband. Boys must …'

'Peace, woman! Wulfwin is not a child and he must learn right from wrong.'

The hall was hushed and Gildas, who had been listening to the exchange, got up from his seat by the hearth. 'Good master! Will you hear me?'

Lord Godric nodded to the old friend who had so many times given him good counsel.

'Let young Wulfwin see a way to right the wrong, if wrong there is. Let us set this girl a riddle for us all to name. If she can do it and we can't guess the answer, let her have the pigs.'

The chief looked doubtful. 'She's only a poor churl from the forest, Gildas. She won't have the words.'

The Riddler reached into the bag of prized beaver-skin which hung round his neck. From it he took a necklace of brightly coloured beads and dangled them in front of Alda's face.

'Look at this necklace, child.
Think of words as if they were beads.
Collect your words together

and thread them on a string.
Play with them
until they sit happily beside each other
in a pattern.

It's not easy. Go home and practise.'

The chief waved his hand. 'Go home, girl. Practise by your hearth and come back tomorrow night. If I can't solve your riddle, you can have your pigs.'

As Alda was led away to join her father and mother, old Gildas followed. Handing the necklace of beads to Alda, he said, 'Take this. It will remind you of my art. But practise!'

CHAPTER SIX

A bright, full moon and hundreds of twinkling stars lit up the sky, as the churls walked back to their home in the forest. Alda trudged along thinking only of the riddle she had to make up for lord Godric.

Looking up to the sky, she murmured, 'The moon! I could have the moon for my riddle.'

She began to work out the words. 'In my yellow dress …' No, that was too much like the swan riddle.

As she stumbled over some loose stones, her father's voice interrupted her thoughts.

'Look where you're going, girl.' He spoke roughly. 'This is no time to be star gazing. Hurry now!'

Her mother took Alda's arm. 'You saw Alfric, child!'

'Alfric!' Alda sounded startled, for she was thinking about riddles. 'Why, yes mother. I saw Alfric. We all did.'

As they edged their way along the river bank, her mother persisted with her thoughts of Alfric.

'You saw the look on his face when we left the Meeting House,' she said. 'You saw the tears in his eyes.'

Alda's father turned his head. 'Hurry, can't you!'

'Husband!' The wife insisted. 'You saw Alfric!'

'Peace, woman! The boy's well placed.'

'But he's so fearful,' she went on, her voice trembling. 'Can't you understand?'

'The boy's slow! You know that! Besides, he gave us no help.'

Alda caught up with her father. 'That's not fair. Alfric told me where to find the pigs.'

But he grumbled on, 'He could have done

more.' Looking back at his wife, he called, 'Hurry now! It's late and the girl must make the riddle.'

Trailing behind them, half crying, the woman mumbled, 'The boy's afraid. I know! I know!'

At last they reached the marsh and the path that led to their hut in the forest. Tall trees hid the stars and only thin shafts of moonlight slipped through the branches. Trees! Alda gazed up at their old trunks. Could she have one of them for her riddle?

As they reached their hut in the clearing, they heard the goat, waiting to be milked. It bleated a soft greeting. Between them they rolled the keeper stone away from the door and went inside. The earth floor was damp and there was a stench of goat. After the warmth and light of the Meeting House, it seemed a poor, cold place.

Alda sat down on her stool and waited for her father to make a fire. It was slow to come tonight, but at last there was a spark. Her father blew gently. There was a little flame and her mother lit a candle from it.

All the family lived together in this one-roomed hut. At one end, alongside Alda's narrow bed with its straw pallet, the goat was tethered. On the other side was her parents' sleeping place. Some wooden bowls and a chipped jug stood on the rough bench against the far wall, next to the loom and the spindle whorls.

The fire began to take hold in the earth hearth and Alda's father threw on some logs. They were damp and sizzled angrily before smoke billowed out over the room. Coughing wearily he fetched a few dry sticks, placed them carefully under the unwilling logs and stood back. Almost at once the fire crackled into life and grey smoke curled slowly up to the hole in the roof thatch.

Alda's father studied her bent head. 'Now, girl! Sit there and make the riddle.'

Alda stared into the fire. 'I don't know if I can do it, father.'

'Don't know!' His voice was impatient. 'Without our pigs we shall starve.' He paused and then added, 'If you'd been watching them!'

'But I couldn't have stopped Wulfwin and his gang.' She was tired and gave a little sob.

Her mother, who was drawing milk from the goat into a wooden bowl, said, 'Leave her, husband.' Then she got up and handed the bowl to Alda. 'Drink this, child! Maybe it will give you strength.'

Alda drank greedily. She'd had nothing to fill her belly since leaving home with the pigs that morning.

Her father brought his stool to the fire and stared at his daughter. He'd never understood her. She had strange ways, quite unlike poor, slow Alfric.

Then he spoke: 'You have to get our pigs back, girl. You must!'

'My head is full of riddles, father.' Her voice was despairing. 'But they are all too simple.'

Her mother came and put a hand on Alda's head. 'Remember the old Riddler, child. What did he say?'

Alda sighed. 'He said, "Think of each word as if it is a bead." Then he said that I must thread the words together in a kind of string.' She put her hand up to the necklace which she'd hung round her neck, and fingered the beads.

Her father shifted restlessly on his stool. 'Go on then, girl. Do it!'

'But, it's not just the words.' She edged her stool away from his. He made it sound easy, but she had to make up a riddle that lord Godric couldn't solve.

Her mother came over to the fire with another bowl of milk. 'Here husband! Have your supper.'

'Is that all I get? A bowl of goat's milk!' A bitter expression crossed his face. 'Alfric, now! He eats bread and meat each day.'

His wife smiled a little. 'Aye, husband.' She was glad to know that, however poorly she fared herself. 'Aye, husband! Our Alfric is a loaf-eater now.'

Alda turned from the fire, gazed at her mother and said, 'A *loaf-eater*.'

She jumped to her feet, excitement in her voice. 'So Alfric is not Alfric, or boy, or churl. Alfric is a *loaf-eater*.'

Her father grunted. 'What has that to do with the riddle,' he complained. A surly expression crossed his face. 'All this talk's a waste of time,' he muttered.

'No, father! It's not. I know what I must do. When I've thought of something for my riddle, I must describe it as something else. I know the way now, so perhaps I can win back the pigs.'

Her father ran his fingers through his hair, saying, 'Perhaps! It's always *perhaps* with you.'

Alda sat down on her stool and stared into the fire. 'I must choose something like a ...' she began softly.

'Like a sword or a shield,' said her father.

'No, father! I don't know about weapons. I must make my riddle about something that I know well.'

Except for the munching of the goat, there was silence in the hut.

Then Alda's mother timidly touched her daughter's arm. 'Make a riddle about a bird, child. You know about birds.'

As the fire ebbed away, Alda smiled to herself. 'Yes! It could be a bird. A magpie, perhaps?' She laughed aloud. 'A magpie could be called "a thief", like Wulfwin!'

'You stupid brat! Have you lost your wits? Her father looked at Alda in exasperation.

'Don't speak of thieving to lord Godric. Young Wulfwin may be in the Meeting House. We must never offend our lords, never!' He blew on the dying embers of the fire. 'Anyway, magpies bring misfortune and we've had too much ill luck.'

His wife nodded. 'Aye, husband,' she said sadly. 'We've had enough trouble in this family.'

Alda got up from her stool. 'I'll away to my bed and practise like the Riddler said.'

Her mother tugged at her daughter's arm. 'Make a bird riddle, child. You could do that.'

'Aye, mother! But I shan't tell anyone what it is. Telling could bring bad luck.'

CHAPTER SEVEN

Next morning Alda was wakened by the goat licking her face. She lay still and went over her riddle. Yes, she had it now.

When the fire was alight and her mother had made their gruel, Alda got up and went over to her stool.

Her father glared at her. 'Is it done, girl? The riddle! Have you got it?'

Alda nodded. She sat down, warmed herself and then ate her food in silence.

With no pigs to watch over, the day went slowly. From time to time Alda said the riddle to herself, but she didn't change it. And she'd tell it to no-one until she stood before lord Godric.

It was getting dark when they crossed the

bridge into the village. Some young thanes, throwing clods of earth at the Great Oak, recognized Alda and jeered.

'Pig-girl! Pig-girl!' they called. One clod narrowly missed Alda's head, but there was no sign of Wulfwin amongst her tormentors and no-one barred their way.

Her father pulled her along behind him and pushed open the door of the Meeting House. Peering through the smoke, they could see lord Godric and his thanes seated at the Ale Board across the far end of the hall. Serving women hurried about, carrying bowls of bread, pitchers of ale and roasted meats.

Alda's father turned to his wife. 'Smell it, woman,' he said enviously. 'Roast venison!'

Alda had never tasted venison and she stared in astonishment as a thane cut a chunk of meat from the joint and tossed it into the air. Two hunting dogs leapt up to seize it in their teeth and banged their heads together before fighting for the prize under the Ale Board.

'Did you see that?' muttered her father. 'Even the thanes' dogs eat better than we poor churls.' He turned to Alda and pushed her forward. 'Go on, girl! Tell someone we've come.'

Alda looked through the smoke for the Riddler. At last old Gildas saw her, pulled himself up from his stool and padded slowly to her side.

'So you've come, child,' he said.

Alda's voice was scarcely more than a whisper: 'Yes, master Riddler.'

He took her shaking fingers. 'Don't be afraid. Come!'

When they reached the Ale Board, lord Godric put down his drinking horn.

'Well, girl,' he said, his eyes twinkling, 'What do you want of me tonight?'

'The pigs, my lord! I've come for the pigs. I've made the riddle as you said.'

Lord Godric guffawed and turned to one of his thanes. 'Stand her up on the Riddler's stool for us all to see and we'll hear what she's done.'

Two strong hands seized Alda's waist, spun her round in the air and then set her down on the stool.

She looked down at the sea of faces. Supposing she couldn't remember the words? Her mouth went dry and she began to tremble.

'Go on, girl!'

It was her father's rough voice. She could see him standing beside her mother at the hearth. How pale and tired they looked. Then she looked up at the ceiling. Candles, mounted on wooden wheels and suspended from the rafters, lit up a deer's skull. Could it bring her luck? She fixed her eyes on the empty shell, licked her lips and began:

'Open your ears
and tell me,
if you can,
what it is
that I am.

Before I was born,
my mother left me
in some stranger's home.
Another mother fed me
as if I were her own.

There, in her tender care
I grew … and grew.
Until, no longer loved,
I was pushed out,
not wanted.

Now, friendless and lonely
I journey to far distant lands,
calling my haunting cry.
Who is it for?
And will I too desert my child one day?

What do you say?'

Alda looked over to the chief, willing him not to answer.

Lord Godric frowned and turned to his wife: 'This is a woman's riddle. What do you say, Hilde?'

Hilde shook her head. 'I don't know,' she said, 'but what kind of mother would leave her infant in some stranger's home?'

The hall was quiet and then a voice called out, 'No creature can be abandoned *before* it's born.'

'The girl's a fool!' It was Wulfwin.

Lord Godric scowled at his son. 'Hold your tongue, Wulfwin. Remember that yesterday you brought dishonour to our name.'

As Wulfwin slunk away, an old thane, seated at the far end of the Ale Board, banged on the table.

'My lord! I have it! That mother! She could have abandoned her unborn child inside an *egg*!'

Alda's heart sank. He was getting near. She jumped down from the stool and flung herself at the Ale Board. 'My lord! It's not an egg.' She leant over the table, her face almost touching lord Godric's. 'It's not an egg! So do I have the pigs?'

Lord Godric stroked his beard, took a long draught from his drinking horn and said slowly, 'Not yet! Say your riddle again, girl.'

Alda felt angry. He'd promised. He'd said that if he couldn't solve her riddle she could have the pigs. She grabbed the chief's arm and cried: 'That's not fair! Is that how lord Godric keeps his promise?'

There was a stunned silence in the hall. Alda's father pushed his way through the thanes gathered before the Ale Board and reached for his daughter.

'Hold your tongue, brat,' he hissed.

'No! Leave her, man!' The chief held up a hand. 'She's done well enough. Give us your answer, girl.'

Alda took a deep breath. 'It's … it's a *cuckoo*.'

All eyes turned to lord Godric as he fingered the silver mount on his drinking horn.

Slowly he nodded his great head. 'A cuckoo! Well, I shall keep my word. You have the pigs.'

Alda closed her eyes. She'd won.

The thanes seated at the Ale Board banged on the wooden planks in approval.

Pushing a wooden bowl of ale towards Alda's

father, lord Godric said, 'Here, man! Drink to your daughter.'

The churl, still grey with all that had gone before, took the bowl in both hands. He put it to his mouth, gulped down a hasty draught and then handed the bowl to Alda. 'We have our pigs, girl. Drink to that.'

Then turning back to the chief, he bowed his bent back. 'You've brought honour to your good name, lord Godric. It will be remembered.'

The chief's wife beckoned to Alda's mother, who was still standing meekly by the hearth.

'Come to the Ale Board, woman. Now, tell me! What is your daughter's name?'

'We call her Alda, my lady.'

Lady Hilde nodded graciously and smiled. 'Alda! The name becomes the girl. Tell me, have you other children?'

The churl woman's eyes clouded. 'You have my son here, my Alfric,' she replied.

Hilde's smile faded. 'That boy! He's so slow. Indeed, Alfric was a bad bargain.' She studied Alda carefully and then looked over to her husband. 'Would we had this girl in our household instead of Alfric.'

Lord Godric turned to Alda's father. 'The lady Hilde would find a place for your daughter here. What do you want for her, man?'

Alda's mother gave an anguished cry. 'My Alda! She's not for sale.' Grasping the wooden Board, hands shaking, she went on, 'You have my son, my Alfric. Isn't that enough?'

Alda's father shook his head. 'The girl's needed in the forest, my lord. Without Alfric there's much work each day.'

The chief thought for a moment, then he said, 'We could trade the pair of them. Where's the boy? *Alfric*!'

Alfric was pushed forward.

'What do you say, boy? Would you leave your sister here in our household and go back to the forest?'

Alfric's heavy face lit up. He looked to his mother and then to his father. 'Why, yes, my lord,' he mumbled.

Lord Godric turned to Alda. 'What do you say, girl?'

Bewildered, Alda covered her face with her hands. 'I don't know,' she whispered. 'How can I know?'

'Don't be afraid, child.' Alda felt a hand on her shoulder and looked up to see the old Riddler standing beside her.

Gildas leant over the Ale Board to lord Godric and said quietly, 'Master! I'm old now in years and this girl has a gift for words. If she came here to the lady Hilde's household, she could learn the craft of riddling from me before I die.'

There were gasps of astonishment from the thanes seated on either side of their chief. A forest girl! A churl! To learn the ancient craft of riddling!

Lord Godric raised his great eyebrows and looked at Alda. 'What do you say, girl?'

Alda lifted her head high. 'I would like to try, my lord,' she said proudly.

'So be it!' Lord Godric looked kindly at Alda's mother. 'Be at peace, woman! On my good name, no harm shall come to Alda.'

He turned next to her father and held out his hand. 'The bargain's struck, man!' Then, giving a short laugh he added, 'One day, perhaps, you will be proud of your daughter and we thanes may have a churl from the forest to be our Riddler.'

PLACES TO VISIT

West Stow, Bury St Edmunds, Suffolk
Saxon Hut

Greensted Juxta-Ongar, Essex
Anglo-Saxon Wooden Church

Bradford-on-Avon, Wiltshire
St. Laurence Church

Ilkley, West Riding, Yorkshire
Anglo-Saxon Crosses

Powys, Wales
Earthworks – Knighton
Offa's Dyke – Presteigne

Wareham, Dorset
Ramparts and St Martin's Church

Winchester, Hampshire
King Alfred's Statue

The British Museum, London
Anglo-Saxon Chronicle, Sutton Hoo Treasures and other Relics

The Ashmolean Museum, Oxford
King Alfred's Jewel

The Jorvik Centre, York
Viking Exhibition